Woman Chief

The Dial Press   New York

WOMAN CHIEF
by Rose Sobol

Library of Congress Cataloging in Publication Data
Sobol, Rose.   Woman Chief.
Summary: Fictional account based on contemporary
writings of Woman Chief, chief of the Crow Indians who
struggled for recognition as a hunter, warrior, and leader.
1. Woman Chief—Juvenile fiction. [1. Woman Chief—
Fiction. 2. Crow Indians—Fiction. 3. Indians of
North America—Fiction] I. Title.
PZ7.S68525Wo   [Fic]   76-2289
ISBN 0-8037-9655-2

To Don with love

Foreword

This is a true story. There once was an Indian woman who became a chief of the Crows.

The title of chief was not awarded her as an affectionate nickname or because she performed one or two bold deeds. She earned the rank by performing many deeds over many years, and despite her sex. Had she been born a man, she would have risen to tribal leadership years sooner. Few men, if any, could match her as a hunter or warrior.

The outline of her life is recorded in the journal of Edwin Thompson Denig. A fur trader for twenty-five years, Denig knew her personally. His manuscript was edited by John C. Ewers and published as a book, *Five Indian Tribes of the Upper Missouri*, in 1968.

To tell her story and make it breathe, I have introduced dialogue. Background details and gaps in Denig's account were filled in after consulting many works about Crow life. Particular acknowledgment is herewith given to the writings of Robert H. Lowie.

Some readers may be offended that I have not detailed at length the nonviolent side of Crow society. During Woman Chief's lifetime the Crows were nomadic hunters and, therefore, a military people. Their culture and religion were intertwined with warfare. What follows, then, is not a treatise on the day-to-day aspects of Crow life. Tribal customs not relevant to Woman Chief's story have been omitted, and peaceful pursuits have been included only where pertinent. Woman Chief was not a medicine man, bride, maker of arrowheads, berry picker, quill worker, or tobacco planter. She was a hunter and warrior.

Other women have dressed themselves briefly in "manly" courage and ridden to battle. Woman Chief made horsemanship and weapons a way of life. She took to the warpath as a leader, and young braves were eager to serve under her.

Woman Chief! It is a name remarkable in its singularity and the only one by which we know her. I have therefore added an earlier name of my own—Lonesome Star. It seems right for all those years when she refused the traditional duties of women and chose instead the hard and lonely path toward glory.

ROSE SOBOL

MIAMI, FLORIDA

1976

Woman Chief

I

It was beginning to be evening, but still early, when Lonesome Star saw the cloud of dust in the distance. It grew rapidly until she made out several riders galloping at breakneck speed.

"They are doing foolish tricks," she told herself, refusing to worry or let anything spoil her day.

She held the bird tighter, and its weight felt good in her hand. It was only a small bird, really. She had shot it at the creek where she had been shooting at rabbits and porcupines since early morning. How surprised Grandfather would be!

Last night he had let her have her first sharp arrows and a wrist guard of buffalo rawhide, for she was nearly ten and growing fast. Now she carried her first kill. She glowed all over, imagining the welcome awaiting her at Grandfather's lodge.

He would seat her in the back, the place of honor. Then Grandmother, who was little and fat and good to her, would wiggle her nose. She would say they must make a feast for the great hunter.

Grandmother would invite some old women and men to come over and eat. Afterward Lonesome Star would make a kill-talk like a mighty hunter. The old women would rejoice and sound the tremolo, tapping their hands against their mouths—*whoo-whoo-whoo*. The old men would smile their praise.

Lonesome Star felt she must reach Grandfather's lodge quickly before she burst with pride. She quickened her step to an easy, smooth trot.

Ten or twelve women were outside the village digging wild turnips. As Lonesome Star passed them, she suddenly felt strange. It wasn't shortness of breath. She was a tireless runner; none of the boys her age could keep up with her for long. It was something else. For a moment everything seemed to stop—the sun in the sky, the wind blowing among the spring leaves, the women as they bent over the earth. The whole world stood silent, motionless. In that empty, bottomless instant she thought, Something terrible is going to happen.

The spell was broken by a cry. It came from the direction of the camp—a shrill and terrifying alarm.

The turnip diggers straightened, their faces frozen with horror. They stumbled and began to run. The younger women dragged the older.

Lonesome Star raced to a wooded rise from which she could look down upon the camp. It was all dust and cries and motion. She lay flat on her belly and stared with her mouth open, hardly breathing.

The people of her tribe, the Gros Ventres of the Prairie, had left their tepees and were running everywhere. Some warriors were chasing their ponies. Others were defending their families against the enemy raiding party.

"Crows!"

The speaker was Chasing Deer, who had been with

the turnip diggers. Born a Crow, Chasing Deer had been captured by the Gros Ventres of the Prairie during the raid in which Lonesome Star's father had been killed six years ago.

"There are too many of them," Chasing Deer said. She moved closer and crouched beside the girl.

Lonesome Star tried to make out what was happening. Everything was mixed up. Crow warriors swarmed among the tepees, killing Gros Ventre men with spears and knives and war clubs while the women fled with the children toward the creek. Sometimes a defender knocked a Crow off his horse and beat him. Lonesome Star saw a Crow cut off a Gros Ventre's arm and ride away with it.

As dusk settled slowly over the battle, the noises changed. Fewer and fewer were the war yells of the defenders. The cries of the women and children had disappeared completely.

"It is nearly over," said Chasing Deer. "In a little while the Crows will be done. They will gather the horses and women and children."

"I will never be taken!" exclaimed Lonesome Star. "I will run and live in the mountains until I am big enough to make war!"

"It is no use," said Chasing Deer. "But do not be

afraid. Crows treat captive women and children as if they were their own. Stay close to me. You will be safe."

Lonesome Star shook her head stubbornly, though she knew she was helpless. She fought back tears and shock. She made herself gaze at the camp below, as if by force of will she could save her grandfather. He was there somewhere, calling to the young warriors to give them courage.

Flames leaped up where the enemy had set fire to the tepees. Soon the entire camp was burning, and the only sound was the chorus of Crow victory shouts.

"I must hide," said Lonesome Star. She picked up her bird so that she would have something to eat. Her hand trembled. "The night will protect me, and I am a good runner."

"You cannot run from a horse," said Chasing Deer. "Listen!"

Over the shouting they heard the clap of hoofs.

A mounted brave, appearing like a great dark spirit among the shadowy trees, blotted out the moon. He leaned forward and reached out a long arm painted with red streaks of lightning.

Lonesome Star was quick and surefooted, but she managed only three strides before he had her. His fingers twisted in her hair and jerked. She cried out in pain.

The small bird slipped from her hand and dropped softly upon the ground.

2

During the journey to the Crow village Lonesome Star
did not cry. Most of the women and girls wept, and
even some of the boys. Lonesome Star looked upon
their crying with scorn.

The first day on the trail she learned that all the
men of her village had been killed. Her grandfather

was dead, and soon she was parted from her grandmother. That evening the Crows divided the spoils of the raid, and her grandmother was taken off to a different camp.

After that night Lonesome Star was never entirely a little girl again.

She gave no sign of her grief. She set her face like stone. She had never known her mother, who had died giving her birth. After the death of her father, there had been Grandmother and Grandfather to comfort her and care for her. Now she was alone, but she hid her sorrow.

For days she spoke only when she was spoken to, and then no more than was necessary. Silence was her only defense, the means by which she guarded her pride.

Around her the Crows bragged of their victory and made sport of the prisoners. Lonesome Star understood most of the boasts and jests, for the language of the Crows and the Gros Ventres was similiar. The two nations had formerly been one.

The story of the split had been Lonesome Star's favorite. Many winter nights when the family was sitting by the fire or lying down, she had pressed her grandfather until he told it again. Every five or six sentences she would cry out, "Yes!" to let him know she had not fallen asleep.

Now she thought of the story as she tramped with the captive women and children. It strengthened her for the trials that might lie ahead.

Long ago, her grandfather had said, the nation dwelt on the prairie and was ruled by two chiefs, each with his followers. At a great buffalo hunt the wives of the two chiefs fell to quarreling over a choice piece of buffalo cow. The argument began with heated words, came to blows, and then to knives. In the fight one of the wives was killed.

The nation divided. Half stood behind one chief, half behind the other. A battle took place in which braves died on both sides. Afterward one chief led his followers from the prairie and up into the mountains. This half became known as the Crows.

The story moved Lonesome Star strangely. Two women had fought like warriors and changed a nation! Lonesome Star thrilled at the boldness and courage of both women. She would wait tensely, burning with anticipation, for Grandfather to reach the part about the knife fight. Then she would cry, "Yes!" after almost every sentence.

When the story ended for the night, she would fall

into a charmed sleep. Scarcely had her eyes closed before she was dreaming of proving that women could do harder tasks than cooking and fetching water and firewood. In her dreams she was a grown-up hunter and warrior.

Only now, in the cruel daylight, she was a child and a captive.

After three days the Crow war party reached camp.

Lonesome Star vowed never to accept the ways of the enemy. She was a Gros Ventre! She would never give in!

She might as well have vowed to crush water.

The Crows made her welcome. Whereas many other tribes normally dashed in the brains of the enemy's women and children, the Crows—like her own Gros Ventres—never misused them. The women prisoners were married to Crow braves and worked beside the other wives. The children were adopted.

Sharp Knife, the Crow brave into whose family she came, was a respected leader and the band's arrow maker. His lodge was painted with bright pictures of his coups. He took an interest in the withdrawn young girl, and he treated her with fatherly kindness and patience.

"You work hard and you work well," he said one morning while she was helping dress hides.

"I do what I am told," she answered.

"You would rather draw water and dress hides and make clothing than play?" he said, regarding her steadily.

"I do not like girls' games," she replied. "They are silly."

"You must learn cooking and crafts," said Sharp Knife. "Otherwise, no one will want you for a wife."

"I do not wish to be like other wives."

"So?"

"When I have a man, I shall ride by his side."

Sharp Knife smiled. "What else do you wish?" he asked kindly.

Lonesome Star hesitated before answering.

It took all her nerve, but she said, "I wish to be a hunter. I wish to go on raids. When I am grown, I shall steal a horse hitched inside an enemy village!"

The words tumbled out. Right afterward she felt ashamed to have bared her secrets. Stealing a picketed horse—along with leading a successful raid, being the first to touch an enemy, and snatching a foe's weapon —was a main coup, or feat of honor, among the Crows.

She expected Sharp Knife to chuckle over her confession. He did not. For a long time he studied her in puzzled thoughtfulness.

"Go and play," he said. "There is a game about to start. Let me see you capture a small horse."

Lonesome Star followed his gaze. Some girls had set up a circle of tiny tepees and were playing at moving camp. They had buckskin dolls stuffed with grass in toy cradles and were putting them on toy pony drags.

Some distance away a group of boys was playing at killing Blackfeet.

"They will tire of killing," remarked Sharp Knife. "Then they will raid the girls' village."

"Will there be a fight?" inquired Lonesome Star with interest.

"No, the boys will be captured," said Sharp Knife. "The girls will hitch them to the drags and make believe they are horses."

"The boys will let them?"

"Yes—all but Red Bull," replied Sharp Knife. "He is too proud."

He handed Lonesome Star a rawhide rope. His voice lowered. "If it is a hunter you will be, capture Red Bull and hitch him properly."

Obediently Lonesome Star joined the girls. The little village had to be moved out of "enemy country," but all at once no enemy was to be seen. The boys were crawling on their bellies along the ground.

When they were close to the girls, they jumped and charged all together, shouting and holding sunflower stalks as spears. It was a noisy fight, with a lot of running and dodging. The victory went to the boys.

"You have stolen all our horses, you bad boys!" cried the girls. "Now you must be our horses and move our camp!"

They threw ropes around the boys. The boys let them, laughing to one another.

But Red Bull stood apart, unsmiling. He was a broad-shouldered youth, and it was obvious already that he would one day make a fine warrior. Lonesome Star took a deep breath and walked straight up to him.

"You are just a horse," she exclaimed. "You are going to pull a drag like the others!"

"I am not a woman's horse," he retorted.

He skipped away and stopped, teasing her, challenging her to catch him.

Lonesome Star gave chase. He was taller and his longer legs helped. For short distances, he was faster.

He would sprint a little way and wait for her to catch up, taunting her. When she drew close, he grinned and sped off.

They stopped and started many times, but Lonesome Star would not quit. Red Bull began to look over his shoulder as he ran, and he no longer grinned or hurled taunts. He stopped more and more often, but not to let her come close. He was panting heavily, and his legs trembled.

Lonesome Star smiled to herself, knowing she was the stronger one now. She stalked him carefully, cutting him off, turning him, making him take the direction she wished. Slowly she worked him back toward the girls' village. He was like a wild horse being herded.

She was swinging her rawhide rope and still breathing easily when he sagged to the ground, worn out, beaten. Her rope fell around his neck. He said nothing, but his eyes pleaded with her not to tell.

She did not, gleeful though she was to have mastered him. She led him to the village with gentle tugs. They both started laughing and joking to make the other children believe he had given up willingly. Some of the girls dashed out and poked their fingers into his sides, couping him.

Lonesome Star ordered him down on all fours. He knelt nervously, his lips forced into a smile. Out of the corner of his eye he watched her hitch him to the drag poles and tie on a tepee with strips of deerhide.

He did his best to fall in with the play and so hide his shame. But he had never been a horse before. He overdid it, rearing and snorting and prancing in place. Lonesome Star patted his rump and crooned to him until he acted as tame as the other young horses.

Sharp Knife observed all this. He said nothing, however, until evening. Then he called her into the lodge.

"You have done well, daughter," he said, laying a hand upon her shoulder. "You have bested the leader of the boys."

He told her to bathe and smoke herself with incense before entering the lodge again.

When she had done as he bid, he painted her yellow all over and stuck a red eagle feather in her hair. Next he slanted two red lines across her arms.

"One line is to give you luck in coups and the other in capturing horses," he explained. "These things are held highest by the Crows. Someday when you have performed great deeds, you shall have a new name, and it shall be honored among our people forever."

3

Lonesome Star kept Red Bull's secret. The other children never learned that he had been forced to play
horse.

She wondered if he would seek revenge. She tried
not to worry about it. Fear was not the way of a warrior, and a warrior she was determined to become.

Sharp Knife encouraged her and reared her as a boy. Her boyish conduct puzzled everyone else. The women thought she was peculiar. The men thought she was too spirited.

Sharp Knife heeded neither the women nor the men. The girl longed to make a name for herself and even wear the white war bonnet. Why not? He helped her with her dream. Patiently he trained her to raid the enemy, defend the camp, and—above all else—hunt.

The Crows were hunters. The land over which they moved ran through the Rocky Mountains. Much of it was the best hunting country in the world.

In 1815, the year of Lonesome Star's capture by the Crows, a few white trappers dwelt in the area. Unlike most tribes, the Crows let them alone. There was still enough game for everyone. Herds of buffalo covered the plains. Along the Yellowstone River elk and deer roamed. Antelope and bighorn sheep and grizzly bear were seen by the hundreds.

For a young hunter learning the use of bow and arrow, the time and place were ideal. Sharp Knife made the girl the finest arrows she had even seen. If she lost one, he did not scold her. He gave her a new one.

One evening about a year after she became a Crow, he discovered her huddled in the tepee, her body quivering with dry sobs. Her arrows had missed their marks all day, and she was tired and frustrated from trying.

He moved slowly about the tepee, acting as if he were alone, ending up, as if by accident, sitting beside her. He touched her knee.

It was a touch that conveyed his meaning more clearly than words. It said, "Do not doubt yourself. I believe in you, and I will help you overcome your weakness. Am I not your father?"

She lifted her head to thank him, and her lips formed the words, "Sharp Knife." She had always called him by name, for she had vowed never to call anyone "Father" again.

His eyes met hers and she saw the love in them. All at once her vow seemed foolish. She threw her arms around his neck and hid her face against his chest.

"Father," she whispered. "Oh, Father . . ."

He took her in his arms and hummed softly. He held her close and hummed to her until she fell asleep.

In the chill morning when she started off to hunt, she felt the comfort of his arms still. She did not need the sun to warm her.

Day after day she practiced her marksmanship on

birds and rabbits and other small game. When she had learned to make every arrow count, Sharp Knife let her go after large animals.

By her twelfth summer she was hunting farther and farther from camp. Alone and on foot she would seek out a waterhole. There, lying motionless, she listened to the leaves. When they moved, rustled by an animal coming to drink, her bow and arrow moved too. She was killing elk and deer and bighorn sheep before any boy her age. She butchered the meat herself and carried it home on her back.

In time she was accepted by the band. The men and women ceased offering Sharp Knife advice on the care and upbringing of a daughter. The bigger boys treated her like one of themselves. When she was not hunting or guarding horses, she joined them in their play.

Archery was strictly a boy's game, but Lonesome Star showed herself the equal of any. Only Red Bull could send an arrow farther. And only he was as good at piercing a grass bundle tossed into the air. One day during her fourteenth year a harder contest was invented to decide who was the best shot. A large hole was drilled in the center of a buffalo chip. The chip was rolled down a hill. Twice Red Bull failed to shoot an arrow through the moving target. Lonesome Star succeeded with her second shot.

"It is just a game," grumbled Red Bull. "Blackfeet and Sioux do not lie down and roll on the ground. They shoot back!"

The other boys cried their approval. They were relieved and grateful. Red Bull had put the game into its proper light. A girl had defeated them—but at play. In a real fight a man was still stronger and braver than a woman!

The boys were flushed and eager to prove themselves. Most of them belonged to the Hammers, a military youth club modeled after the tribe's eight adult war clubs. Red Bull did not have to suggest Fighting-on-Horses. Others suggested the game for him. He looked questioningly at Lonesome Star. She had never played before, but his look was a challenge.

"I shall play," she said, though she knew the danger. She had watched the game many times. Fighting-on-Horses was a battle in all but the killing.

The rules were simple. Two sides of mounted "warriors" charged one another. Anyone knocked from his horse was counted as slain. The riders kicked, punched, and wrestled until all the players of one side had been unhorsed.

The two sides formed quickly.

"Take courage!" the boys called to each other. "Take courage!"

The words were those which grown-up warriors used to steady each other in war. "Take courage! Take courage! It is a good day to die!"

The signal was given. From twenty young throats arose a single, solid war whoop.

The two lines thundered together. The horses bumped, reared, and churned up dust. Each boy tried to keep his seat while unseating a foe.

"I will not be the first to fall," Lonesome Star vowed under her breath.

She lost sight of Red Bull and found Little Dog at her side, cursing her madly. He was small and narrow-chested, and usually among the first to be thrown.

"Foolish girl!" he yelled. "You cannot hope to beat a boy!"

"You think I am weak, do you?" she yelled back.

She punched at him furiously, striking his arms and face. A blow smashed into his throat. He squeaked, strangling with pain.

In an instant Lonesome Star seized him by the wrist. She yanked and tumbled him to the ground.

Before she had time to gloat, an arm encircled her

head. She uttered a cry of surprise as she was pulled from her horse.

It was Red Bull. She had been watching for him. But he, waiting his chance, had taken her from behind. She beat against his arm, struggling in helpless fury.

He rode a few paces, holding her in the headlock and letting her dangle. Then he changed his grip and hauled her across his lap. She was now bent backward cruelly. Her legs kicked on one side of his horse. Her head and shoulders were pinned on the other.

Red Bull paused to change his grip again, and she was able to glare up at him. At that moment he shook with a roar of laughter. His hand went under her chin and shoved. She was dumped heels over head across his bare thighs and onto the hard ground.

Later she learned that Red Bull had come out a hero. He had not been unhorsed, and his side had won. She did not care. By then she was lying in Sharp Knife's lodge, hurting in every bone.

After dark Scold-the-Dog, one of Sharp Knife's wives—a Crow warrior showed his wealth by the number of his horses and wives—came into the lodge and knelt beside the bruised girl. Scold-the-Dog was in charge of housekeeping. Her tepee poles, always straight and cleanly trimmed, gave her a good name.

"Red Bull is here," she whispered. "He wishes to speak with you."

Lonesome Star got to her feet. She walked outside carefully, hiding her aches.

Red Bull greeted her politely. He was bathed and he wore his best shirt. His hair was greased and dressed in a pompadour with pigtails on each side.

He is good to look upon, Lonesome Star found herself thinking. She understood why many girls were sick with love for him.

"The moon is bright," he said. He seemed ill at ease, and he rubbed his hand on his chest awkwardly. "Many are gathering rhubarb. Will you come?"

"Yes," she answered. "I will come with you."

When they reached the field, they saw many couples. Red Bull stopped in the tall bushes at the field's edge. He had not said a word on the walk, and he had not yet touched her. A girl's giggle came from nearby. He seemed more uncomfortable than ever.

If he is not haughty, I shall let him embrace me, thought Lonesome Star. But he must admit I am as good as he.

"I am sorry for what happened today," he said finally. "It was not fair."

"In war anything is fair," she replied. "I am un-hurt."

"It is right that I say something," he said. "I am stronger than you. You know that."

"You are bigger," she said.

"I am stronger," he repeated dully.

"I am as good as you!"

"No," he answered, and his voice was odd and heavy. "That is what I have to say. You are not as good. You are better."

Without another word he turned and walked toward the village.

Lonesome Star stood rooted in amazement. It was not until much later, when she lay down to sleep, that she realized how much she had won. And how much she had lost.

She could outride and outshoot any boy her age. Red Bull, a leader, had admitted it.

That was what she had won.

And yet . . .

He had taken her to gather wild rhubarb, and they had gathered none. He had not embraced her. He had not even held her hand or touched her.

4

When Lonesome Star reached the age of fifteen, she started going on the great buffalo surrounds. As was the Crow custom, she hunted on horseback with bow and arrow. She used a gun only for hunting on foot when the snow was too deep for a horse to overtake a buffalo.

A few of the strongest braves could send an arrow clean through one of the huge beasts. The girl realized she might never grow to such strength. So she taught herself to kill five or six buffalo at a race and make it look easy.

For the next ten years she hunted buffalo with the young braves and shared their other duties. Still she felt unfulfilled. She was forbidden to go on war parties. Sharp Knife refused to let her, despite her skill as a rider and hunter.

Nevertheless she clung to her dreams. Someday she would go to war. Someday she would count coup over a fallen foe!

In 1831, when she was twenty-six, the American Fur Trading Company built a trading post in the land of the Crows at the mouth of the Rosebud Creek on the Yellowstone River. It was named Fort Cass, and it was a solid, strong fort. It had to be.

Blackfeet and Cheyenne—sworn enemies of the Crows as well as of the whites—were an ever-present menace. White men who left the fort to cut wood, guard horses, or hunt were regularly ambushed by these hostile tribes.

The Crows lived at peace with the whites. Their belief in the superhuman powers of the paleface traders was far stronger than that of other Indians.

Moreover the Crows desperately needed allies. They were a small tribe, numbering about eight hundred lodges, or about five thousand people. Horse raids by more powerful neighbors, principally the Sioux from the east and the Blackfeet from the west, threatened them with destruction. To protect themselves they sided with the white men.

The Crows camped near Fort Cass in the spring and autumn. In the summer they left to trade with the Flathead, Shoshone, and Nez Percé Indians. Then the entire nation moved east to the villages of another friendly tribe. Here they exchanged some of the horses and goods received from the western tribes, along with dried meat, skin lodge covers, and clothing prepared by the Crow women. In return they got corn, pumpkins and tobacco.

Late in the autumn most of the Crows went back to the mountains to chase large game, for they were hunters and cultivated the ground only in connection with their sacred tobacco ceremony. They brought their furs to Fort Cass the following spring. One or two bands, however, usually stayed near the fort throughout the winter.

In 1835 a large war party of Blackfeet attacked the

lodges by the fort. The Crows were surprised, and several men were slain. The rest escaped into the fort, taking most of their horses. Among the survivors was Lonesome Star.

The Crow braves hurried to help the white traders mount a defense at the fort. In the noise and confusion, Lonesome Star slipped away from the women. She climbed to the platform behind the wall and took her place with the men.

The Blackfeet charged twice. Both times they were scattered by arrows, musket fire, and the small cannon atop the fort's two bastions. They regrouped at a safe distance and took council.

During the lull the defenders began to stretch their limbs and walk around. They talked. Their voices, which had been hoarse and loud during the nearness of death, became normal. They joked with relief.

Lonesome Star leaned against the wall. She had tasted war! Her head reeled from the smoke and blasts, but she was alive. She trembled ever so slightly with delight.

Her quiver was half empty. This amazed her. She had not been fully aware of her actions. She was still breathing with excitement when she saw the Blackfeet signaling.

"They want to talk with us," she said to the bearded trader next to her.

On the ground a group of men, both white and Indian, gathered hastily. Sharp Knife was there, and so was Red Bull.

"It is a trick to draw us out," a white man warned.

The others agreed. Still, was it not wise to see what the enemy wanted? One man could go. . . .

The men in the group could not decide. They stood very still while they talked. They seemed fearful of any motion that might draw attention to themselves. Each wished to be as little noticed as possible.

None of them will go, thought Lonesome Star. Not Sharp Knife, not Red Bull.

She turned and looked beyond the wall. The dust had settled, and she saw the Blackfeet clearly.

"I will go," she announced. Her voice shook, and she paused to clear her throat before continuing. "I speak their language."

She made it sound as if she alone were able to understand the enemy. In fact, many of the Crows spoke the Blackfoot tongue, including Sharp Knife and Red Bull.

She got down from the wall and saddled her horse. The fort was hushed. Every eye was on her.

Sharp Knife walked over. In his glance was pride, and a tinge of shame. A woman was undertaking what no man dared. He handed her a white man's pistol.

She accepted it without a word and swung astride her horse. Her heart was racing. Somehow the gates opened in front of her, and she was riding alone.

When she arrived within hailing distance of the enemy, the Blackfeet let out a savage cry of glee. They saw by her clothing she was a woman. Throughout her active life Lonesome Star never dressed as a man.

Five Blackfoot warriors galloped toward her, laughing at the chance for an easy prize. As they approached pistol range, Lonesome Star called to them to halt. They came on, paying no mind to her words.

She drew her pistol and killed the leader.

The other four shrieked with rage and fired back. They missed, for Lonesome Star had become a swiftly moving target. She was riding now as she had taught herself to ride chasing buffalo. There was no time to reload the pistol. She used her bow and arrow.

"*Yea-hey!*" she shouted over and over. She set her shaft, aimed, and released arrow after arrow without slackening speed. Darting this way and that, she slew two more Blackfeet without taking a wound.

One Crow woman was outfighting five Blackfoot

warriors, and the onlookers on both sides reacted. Those in the fort cheered at the top of their lungs. The Blackfeet watched in fury.

The two remaining Blackfeet broke off. Panic had stripped away their courage. This woman was too much for them. They wheeled their horses and fled for their lives.

Like a raging tide the main body of Blackfeet burst toward the solitary female warrior. They fired bullets and arrows and pursued her to the fort.

The white traders and her own people were ready. They kept up a covering fire. The Blackfeet stopped short and retreated. Lonesome Star entered the gates amid screams of joy.

The fighting ended there. The attempt to capture the fort was abandoned. When the sun had lowered to shoulder height, the Blackfeet were gone.

That night Lonesome Star's praises were sung around the campfires. When at last she lay down on a bed of sage, she could not sleep. Her happiness kept her awake.

The next morning she was up at dawn. She went to the walls, triumph in every light-footed step. The daybreak star hung in the sky. A coyote howled. She faced the rising sun.

"Sun," she said. "I slew the Blackfeet. I slew them though the muscles of their shoulders stood out like snakes crawling. Three I slew and two fled before me. You looked down and saw me do it, Sun. I give you thanks."

She lowered her head and turned away, murmuring the first words of an old chant:

Whenever there is trouble,
I shall come through. . . .

Her lips stilled. She raised her head, and her dark eyes gleamed with a new light.

"I have begun," she whispered.

5

The Blackfoot attack called for revenge.

In anger and hatred the band of Crows filed from Fort Cass. Once at their village their mood changed. They beheld what the Blackfeet had left. Grief overcame them.

They knelt on the ground and cried over their dead.

But tears and wailing were not enough. Relatives of the slain warriors cut themselves, slicing off a joint of a finger. Friends hurt themselves as they saw fit. Lonesome Star jabbed her arm till it was wet with blood.

The corpses were wrapped in tepee hides, and the entire camp swore vengeance to the spirits of the dead. Their families then went about the burials—in the forks of trees, on four-pole platforms, among the rocks, or on top of hills. Not until more Blackfeet were killed would the families cease to mourn.

The advisors met within the council tepee in the center of the village, smoked, and decided what action to take.

Lonesome Star learned their decision from Sharp Knife. "We will make war," he said. "A big raid. I am to lead it."

Lonesome Star did not reply. She waited for her ears to hear the words her soul longed for. Sharp Knife finally spoke them.

"You will go along. The advisors desire it. It is my desire as well."

Lonesome Star's breath caught in her throat. Suddenly she felt taller, and her heart was stronger than before. She said nothing however. She had earned the right to fight. It was not to Sharp Knife or the advisors that she must give her thanks.

As soon as she was alone, she walked away from the village, far across the frozen ground. On a small hill she stopped and raised her hands to the sun. Then she stooped and touched the earth, mother of all.

When she got back to the village, she found a great to-do. Everyone was helping to make ready for the raid.

One old man, a relative of a slain warrior, was organizing a Sun Dance, the prayer of revenge. Lonesome Star knew it might last until the raiders returned. She did not join in. She had her own preparations to look after.

For three days the village hummed. The women mended clothing and mixed dried deer meat with dried berries and buffalo tallow. Such a mixture, called pemmican, would keep for years. War parties lived on it when game was scarce.

The men saw to their weapons. Arrows were straightened and sharpened. Bowstrings of buffalo sinew were tested for weaknesses. Bows were filed down for better balance, and the white elk bone repainted.

The night before the war party was to depart, Sharp Knife called Lonesome Star aside.

"You will need a second horse, a war-horse," he said. "Go and pick one."

It was a hoped-for gift. Lonesome Star rode her little mare several miles to where the band's horses were staked. Sharp Knife owned forty-seven.

"Father said you would be coming to choose one," said Long Beaver, Sharp Knife's youngest son. He and three of his brothers guarded the family horses.

Lonesome Star did not hesitate. She walked to a big white-faced bay stallion with white hind legs. For many moons she had fancied him. He was always fat and shiny, even in winter.

She stroked his neck and spoke fondly to him. Then she led him by his bark cord back to camp. She staked him by the lodge beside her mare, which was beginning to grow old.

Many times before the sun set she strolled over to admire him. Even standing still he seemed to rejoice in his strength.

As darkness gathered, she paid him a last visit.

I shall ride you like the wind, she thought.

Footsteps sounded behind her, light and quick. Turning, she saw Little Feather, Red Bull's sister.

The young woman approached timidly. Unlike Lonesome Star, she was not too tall. Her perfect height, slim figure, and straight nose were admired by the Crows, and she was considered beautiful.

"I have made you these," she murmured.

Into Lonesome Star's hands she pressed a pair of moccasins. They were made of soft buckskin sewed to sturdy rawhide soles. Dyed porcupine quills decorated the sides.

Lonesome Star started to speak. But there was no one to hear. Little Feather had fled into the shadows among the lodges.

The birds were singing when the raiders gathered at sunup. The war-horses seemed to understand. They nickered and tossed their heads, happy and eager.

The whole camp turned out to watch the departure. The forty raiders, hung with medicines—sacred objects obtained from medicine men—made their farewells. A great shout lifted as they started off, riding toward the Great Plains, the land of the Blackfeet.

For three days all went well.

Sharp Knife alone had misgivings. He kept them to himself until the fourth night.

"We are too many," he said to Lonesome Star. They were seated in an overnight windbreak of sticks and bark. "Ten or twelve men are best. The advisors are too greedy for revenge."

Sharp Knife spoke truly. Some of the younger braves were already growing restless. They thirsted for quick glory. In battle they might be hard to manage.

They will get out of control if we do not find the enemy soon, thought Lonesome Star.

Tracks were seen in the snow the following morning. Was the enemy near? The snow was old, and it was hard to tell anything.

To be safe, Sharp Knife sent out eight scouts—the men who were bravest and most experienced in war. After they had gone ahead, the sky darkened.

Snow fell. The main body bundled up and kept on. Eventually the snow let up. But a cold wind blew harshly. To Lonesome Star the cold was of little concern. She worried about what lay behind: their tracks in the fresh snow. So many hoofprints were a signal to the Blackfeet.

Late that same evening two of the scouts returned. The other six were a day's ride ahead. They were trailing a small party of Blackfeet.

"Make camp," said Sharp Knife, and ordered the building of four war lodges. He marked the sites at the edge of the timber, where the lodges could not be seen from the open plain.

The men carried no axes on war parties, but the

work progressed rapidly nonetheless. They used their sharp scalping knives to cut poles. These were covered with heavy slabs of bark, making the shelters as sturdy as little forts. Sharp Knife went from shelter to shelter checking that each was weathertight.

Things started going wrong shortly after the war lodges were finished. A driving snowstorm struck. The snow froze hard and the horses could not find forage. Lonesome Star's sleek bay stallion seemed skin and bones. His coat had faded to a brownish black.

Although the warriors put black paint below their eyes to ward off the glare, snow blindness overtook three of the younger warriors. Scratched Face, the son of a medicine man, put snow upon their eyes. He sang a sacred song his father had heard in a dream. Then he blew on the back of their heads, and they saw again.

Several of the spirited younger braves grumbled at Sharp Knife's leadership. They talked of riding off on their own and killing Blackfeet.

By the fourteenth day the pemmican was running low and the atmosphere was tense. The grumbling of the younger braves increased.

Sharp Knife, however, remained calm. He set about making a pile of sticks.

Almost immediately riders were seen. The six scouts were returning. They rode a zigzag course and waved their bows—the signal that a Blackfoot camp had been sighted.

Sharp Knife galloped out to meet them. When he rode back, the rest of the braves were standing around the sticks. Sharp Knife kicked over the pile.

The men scrambled and shouted, "*Yi-hoo!*" To get a stick meant success in the stealing of horses. Sharp Knife had made sure there were enough sticks to go around.

The tension of the days before was released. The men were hopeful again.

A small fire was built in a sheltered area where its glow would not be seen by the enemy. The men gathered around it, warming themselves. Winterberry tea was prepared. They ate pemmican, washing it down with the tea.

The men joked and laughed again. Their faith in the calm and steady Sharp Knife was renewed. They did not object when he ordered them to remain hidden in the war lodges all the next day.

Toward sunset he moved from lodge to lodge. In each he spoke the same words: "It is time to paint your faces."

The younger men brought in the horses. With the darkness of night to protect them, the war party trotted from the woods to take revenge upon the enemy.

6

The Blackfoot village that the scouts had sighted numbered more than one hundred tepees. The Crows approached it in the dead of night.

An attack upon so large a band of the enemy could be costly. Lonesome Star wondered whether Sharp Knife would dare risk it. She wondered, too, what his vision had told him.

That a vision had been given him back at the war lodges she did not question. How else to explain his timing? He had made a pile of sticks before the scouts were even seen. He had known of their return in advance.

Moreover, something troubled him. He had been acting oddly, withdrawn. What else had he glimpsed of the future?

Sharp Knife finished talking with the scouts. He had reached a decision. Wheeling his horse, he rode to Lonesome Star.

"There is a woods downstream of the village," he said. "It is nearer the Blackfoot horses than the tepees. We will attack from there."

The war party rode to the woods, dismounted, and fingered their medicines to bring good fortune. Red Bull and several others had brought pouches of buckskin, each with a tobacco seed inside. Lonesome Star had an elkskin headband, feathered in the back. Sharp Knife smoked a pipe.

At the first light of dawn Sharp Knife put away his pipe and called everyone to him.

"The attack will be against the horses," he said.

He gave instructions slowly, broodingly. A weight seemed to lie upon his tongue. He talked as though describing an action that had taken place already, an action that sorrowed him.

He spoke the names of four of the scouts, but did not look at them.

"Kill the horse guards and run off as many animals as possible," he instructed. "The rest of you must remain here. Be ready in case the enemy gives chase."

Like most Indian warfare the plan was simple and loose. What counted were surprise and the courage of the individual.

Sharp Knife raised his arm and let it flop to his side. "We go."

He led the four scouts out on foot. Lonesome Star watched until they disappeared behind a rise.

After that there was stillness and waiting.

Once Red Bull came to her side. "It will go well," he said. "They will rub out the guards and take many horses."

She did not answer, and he moved away.

She remained facing in the direction Sharp Knife and the scouts had taken, straining her eyes, as if by the power of her concentration she could bring the men through unharmed.

For what seemed a long time, too long, the Crows waited tensely in the woods, listening.

The sun had cleared the horizon when gunshots sounded. Blackfoot guns, for the five Crows had none with them. Hurriedly the band in the woods tightened saddles. Some of the young braves saw the chance to win honors and jumped astride. Lonesome Star and Red Bull were among those braves who tried to stop them.

They went from rider to rider, reminding each that he must obey Sharp Knife's orders to wait.

"It is not the way of the Crow to be reckless," warned Lonesome Star, "or to seek grand battles merely from a thirst for glory."

It was no use. The young braves were determined to count coup.

"Take courage!" they called to each other as they galloped toward the gunfire. "The earth is all that lasts!"

They did not gallop far. They were still in view when they met the herd of stolen horses.

The sudden appearance of the young braves startled the horses. They veered and broke. Before the Crows could get them going in a bunch again, five or six Blackfeet began firing.

The Crows were too many, and the Blackfeet did not advance. But the Blackfoot horse Sharp Knife was riding took an arrow and went down between the two forces.

Lonesome Star reacted quickly. But Red Bull was quicker still. He reached the fallen leader a horse length ahead of her.

Fortune favored Lonesome Star. Red Bull's sorrel tripped, flinging him. Before he had remounted, Sharp Knife was riding double behind the woman warrior.

It was a bold and splendid stunt, turning and rescuing a disabled comrade, though it was always more praised than copied. Lonesome Star's daring was admired on the spot, but the praise due her was postponed. The Crows were busy escaping.

Sharp Knife, now astride one of the captured horses, moved the band crisply and unerringly. He maintained absolute control, speeding men and horses at a pace rare over such distances. He seemed to be everywhere at once. Now he showed the way, now he protected the rear. By the second night, the pursuing Blackfeet had been shaken.

Sharp Knife allowed the men to rest and eat in the half dark. The warriors chewed pemmican, glancing uneasily at their leader. Lonesome Star shared their tension. She kept her eyes on Sharp Knife.

He did not touch food. He sat apart, his gaze turned inward.

Lonesome Star alone had the courage to speak with him.

"We captured sixty horses," she said. "All of them are young and strong."

"We lost Muddy Hand and Crazy Fire," said Sharp Knife. "We did not kill one of the enemy."

There could be no argument, and Lonesome Star did not try to comfort him falsely. She knew as well as he the rule of a successful raid. The number of horses captured—even the number of enemy slain— meant nothing if the price was the life of a single Crow.

"I was sent to kill Blackfeet," said Sharp Knife.

He offered no excuses. He did not tell her what had gone amiss. Later she learned that the Blackfeet had suspected their coming and were not surprised. Against an alerted foe, it was an unbelievable feat to have run off so many horses.

In spite of this, the raid had failed. Two Crows had died. For Sharp Knife the failure meant his downfall.

"You know my vow," he said stonily.

"Yes," replied Lonesome Star. The thought of it made her shudder.

Before departing, Sharp Knife had vowed to kill five Blackfeet—or leave his body in their country. Every step homeward brought him closer to disgrace. There was no way, Lonesome Star thought, of saving his honor.

She was wrong. What no human power could bring about, fate accomplished. As they neared the mountains, Sharp Knife's three scouts galloped in.

They brought amazing news. A small war party of nine Blackfeet had been discovered.

Apparently the Blackfeet had been unsuccessful in finding any Crows and were returning to their village. Discouraged, tired, and hungry, they had grown careless. They had allowed themselves to be seen.

While Sharp Knife listened to the scouts' report, his face showed nothing. But his eyes spoke. They lit like dark fires burning. Fate had thrown into his path a means to recover his standing in the tribe. He took Lonesome Star and twenty other warriors. They set off for the Blackfeet, the dry snow whining under their horses' hoofs.

The battle was brief. The Crows dismounted and shot from ambush. Three Blackfeet fell. The rest spun their horses and fled cursing.

By the time the Crows had untied their own horses

and taken up pursuit, the Blackfeet had too great a lead. Their captain knew the war trail and the old war lodges that dotted it. He got his men into a fortification high in a pine forest.

The Crows urged Sharp Knife to leave the enemy alone now. An attack would endanger more lives. They had already lost Muddy Hand and Crazy Fire.

Sharp Knife didn't seem to hear. He sent for his pack horse with his war suit. Gravely he donned a shirt and leggings fringed with human hair, an eagle-feather war bonnet, and a robe covered with scalps. All this display was like a ceremony. Coming at the end of an unsuccessful raid, it bespoke some deadly purpose. Lonesome Star guessed what the purpose was.

"We must stop him!" she told Red Bull. "He will charge the Blackfeet alone. I'm sure he has had a vision of doom and death."

Red Bull seized the bridle of Sharp Knife's horse. "If we attack, we shall lose more of our people," he pleaded.

Sharp Knife commanded him to let go, but the other braves stood with the young warrior.

Sharp Knife could do nothing. At last he gave in. "Let us go home," he said.

Red Bull released the bridle, and Sharp Knife smiled a strange, faraway smile.

His horse was free, and he made the animal caper as if in sport. Every step carried him a little farther from his warriors and a little closer to the Blackfoot fortification.

Suddenly Lonesome Star realized what was happening. Sharp Knife had outwitted her and everyone else. He was beyond catching.

"Hey-ahey-hey!" he roared, throwing back his head and thrusting his lance toward the sky. "Three Blackfeet cannot pay for the lives of Muddy Hand and Crazy Fire!"

He gathered his war-horse, pulling it in so that its powerful neck coiled and it reared on its hind legs. He drove back his heels, and the animal slammed to earth in full stride. In an instant horse and rider had cleared the Blackfoot barrier of logs and stones.

As he landed amid the enemy, Sharp Knife shouted a terrible shriek of rage. He struck one of the Blackfeet through with his lance before he died, a cluster of arrows in his body.

The Crows stormed after him. They were no longer warriors, they were fiends. Screaming and slashing, they cut down the Blackfeet without taking a wound themselves. Their fury was so great that they ignored coups and scalps. Sharp Knife's last act had banished every thought of personal glory.

They bore his body from the bloody ground. When the weeping was over, they wrapped it and tied it tightly. Four braves started to place it across his horse.

Lonesome Star stopped them. "He vowed to leave his body in the country of the Blackfeet," she said. "Let it be so."

Again his body was taken up, and amid fresh weeping it was laid in the fork of a tree. Then the war party headed for home.

Lonesome Star rode beside Red Bull. During the charge he had knocked her off her horse. She had fallen outside the Blackfoot war lodge and had missed the fighting. Somehow she could not be angry with him. He had sought to keep her from injury. She understood, and she forgave him.

They had topped a wooded summit when she looked back. Her gaze found the tree standing by the Blackfoot war trail, and her thoughts flew to other days. The man who had taken her into his tepee and helped her find her own lonely trail—the man who had never criticized her for being different, only encouraged her to be true to herself—was gone. His bundled form lay in the leafless winter branches.

"Rest, my father, a terror to your enemies even in death," she whispered.

7

"We have chosen you," Red Bull told Lonesome Star as they neared their village. "You were dearest to Sharp Knife. You must break the news."

It was a hard duty—and how different from what she had expected! Before they had taken to the warpath, she had looked forward to this day. She had pictured herself returning a hero among heroes.

Since childhood she had been forced by her sex to be a bystander at the victorious homecomings of others. She had nevertheless felt thrilled to hear about the warriors' deeds and had joined in welcoming them home.

Now, instead of victory, she had failure to report. Instead of joy there would be mourning. She must bring grief to the families of Sharp Knife, Muddy Hand, and Crazy Fire.

She took a gun and blanket and trod heavily to a hill overlooking the village. She pointed the gun straight up and pulled the trigger.

The people stopped what they were doing and looked. Lonesome Star gave the signal of death. For each man killed, she raised the blanket and then let it fall.

Three times she raised it. Three times she let it fall.

Five advisors were sent from the village. They sat with Lonesome Star and questioned her about the disaster.

She spoke of Sharp Knife's able leadership and his last charge. She spoke of the bravery of Muddy Hand and Crazy Fire, and the capture of the Blackfoot horses.

It did no good. She could not make the mission sound successful.

The advisors rose to go.

"Sharp Knife," said one. He spoke the name solemnly, sorrowfully.

While the village mourned, the war party remained in the hills ten days, as was the custom. On the eleventh day, they took to the warpath again.

Lonesome Star led. She had been chosen captain because she was Sharp Knife's daughter. But the men respected her war skills as much as they respected her family tie.

She had dreamed of the honor. She was prepared for it. Remembering Sharp Knife's words about too large a war party, she took only Red Bull and eight others.

Soon she was glad for Little Feather's comfortable moccasins, for the party traveled on foot. Horses had a way of whinnying at the wrong moment, even if their nostrils were held.

For three days they followed a known war trail of the Blackfeet. On the fourth they entered enemy country. They camped that night in the woods flanking a dry creek bed.

With the morning light, they spied a charred spot

of ground, the remains of a campfire, not half a bow shot away.

"Blackfeet were here," said Lonesome Star as she studied the ground. "They moved only a day or two ago."

She named Red Bull and Scratched Face as scouts and sent them to follow the trail. They reported back shortly.

"The Blackfeet are near," said Red Bull. "Seven of them, guarding horses."

"Get ready," said Lonesome Star, and she unfolded her plan. She and Red Bull were to go ahead. The rest were to stay hidden until the first shot.

The two warriors started off by themselves. They made no attempt to sneak up on the enemy. They walked hand in hand, pretending to be sweethearts.

One of the Blackfeet called out to them. He signaled them to approach in peace. The two Crows advanced innocently. They were within range when the Blackfeet realized they were Crows, seized their guns, and fired.

Lonesome Star and Red Bull fired back, and the other Crows raced up. The outnumbered Blackfeet ran into a hollow. The Crows surrounded them.

In desperation the Blackfeet made it a hand-to-hand fight. One of them singled out Lonesome Star.

He leaped for her. She sprang aside and he lunged past, struggling for balance. She took him with her knife.

As he fell, screaming, an arrow pierced his shoulder. Immediately Lonesome Star touched him with her bow, couping him.

Breathless, shaking, she straightened and glanced around. The battle was over. The Blackfeet were down. Her Crows were howling like wolves; they had not lost a man.

"Woman, go and scalp him."

The speaker was Red Bull. He was testing her fitness to lead.

The brave she had wounded was lying on his back. His legs were still kicking.

"He is not through dying," she protested.

"Do it," said Red Bull.

She leaned over. She saw that the Blackfoot was young and strong. He wore a feather in his hair. He was a handsome man.

Lonesome Star started to do it. The Blackfoot looked at her once. He ground his teeth. . . .

"You have pleased your father," said Red Bull approvingly. "Do not cry."

"I am not crying," insisted Lonesome Star. Her eyes glistened brightly. But whether she felt triumph or despair she herself was not sure.

The war party rode home, and they were so excited that no one slept that night. They had captured thirty horses. They had slain seven of the enemy. They had gained revenge.

When they got close to their village, they made camp overnight and lit a fire. After the fire burned out, the charcoal was mixed with buffalo blood. All the braves blackened their faces, for black showed victory. The first brave to strike a coup and the first brave to take a gun blackened their shirts as well.

Just before dawn, they walked to the edge of the village. Lonesome Star shot into the air. As her gunshot had once brought grief, it now brought joy.

Men, women, and children rushed out of the lodges to see the war party lined up in a row with their faces blackened and scalps tied to willow sticks. Women brought out their drums. Beating time and dancing, they led the raiders in a victory parade through the village. Lonesome Star carried her coup stick hung with the scalp and feather. Even those women who had mocked her or been secretly jealous of her shouted praises.

The celebration continued long into the night. The people feasted, sang, danced, and later performed the ceremony of lodge striking by tapping the lodges of the war party with willow sticks. The raiders made kill-talks and gave away the stolen horses to friends and relatives, and to the families of the slain warriors.

Lonesome Star cut up her Blackfoot scalp. She gave pieces to the men so that they would have more scalps to dance with. She gave a horse to Little Feather. Then she retired. She tried to sleep.

It wasn't the singing that kept her awake, or the dancing, or the drums. It was the memory of one look . . . and the sound of teeth grinding.

8

Lonesome Star's daring leadership was sung in the camp for many days. Soon it was known to the whole Crow nation.

Within the year, she led seven young men in another raid against the Blackfeet. Fortune continued to shine on her.

Her war party stole upon the enemy camp at night and ran off seventy horses. The Blackfeet followed and caught up. After a sharp fight, the Crows got away with most of the horses and two Blackfoot scalps.

Lonesome Star killed and scalped one of the Blackfeet with her own hands. Although the other was wounded by her men, she was the first to strike him, and she took his gun while he was still alive.

Such horse raids were a means of survival. Without mounts, the Crows could not live as hunters. The yearly trading with the Flatheads and Nez Percés could supply only enough animals to replace losses from disease, old age, and death. Far larger numbers were lost through theft. Raiders ran off as many as a hundred horses at a sweep. The Sioux stole horses from the Assiniboins, who stole from the Blackfeet. In turn the Blackfeet stole from the Crows, and the Crows from the Blackfeet. Hence a poor beast might come back to its first owner several times. Among the tribes of the upper Missouri River, the Crows were the richest in horses and the cleverest of horse thieves.

What nation began this circle of warfare no one remembered or cared. Each raid called for an answering raid, either to recover horses or avenge a death. Hatred ran high, especially between Blackfoot and Crow. Seldom did seven days go by without small herds being run off from a Crow or Blackfoot camp.

During the years of her thirties, Lonesome Star led many raids against the Blackfeet, the Sioux, and her former tribe, the Gros Ventres of the Prairie. In each she was successful. Although daring, she was never reckless. Her first concern was always with the safety of the men under her.

Her regard for their lives lifted her into the company of the best Crow captains. These were leaders who "never signal a loss." They ranked above leaders who "regularly bring in horses" and leaders who "regularly kill."

Songs in her praise were composed after each of her brave deeds. Young men asked to serve under her. Old men believed she bore a charmed life.

On state occasions it was the tribal custom to strike a post with a stick and retell heroic deeds. Lonesome Star took her turn ahead of many fine warriors. In every battle she added to her fame.

The time finally came when she could no longer be called Lonesome Star. She deserved a more fitting name, a more respected name.

She received it the day after returning from a raid

against the Sioux. She had performed the most daring feat possible. She had cut loose and stolen a Sioux horse picketed near its owner's tepee.

With this accomplishment, she had performed the fourth of the four highest coups, or tests of courage. Already she had been the first to strike in battle. She had been the leader of a successful raid. She had snatched a gun in a hand-to-hand fight. Now she had stolen a horse within an enemy camp.

Each coup meant a step toward chieftainship. A "chief" was simply a warrior who had succeeded in the four feats at least once. Lonesome Star had earned the title.

A crier came to her. He bid her come to the council lodge.

She was expecting him. She had on her best elkskin dress. Little Feather had trimmed it with locks of hair. Each lock represented a coup. Wolf tails were fixed to the heels of her moccasins.

At the council lodge all the advisors and warriors were gathered. Lonesome Star sat down in the place of honor. She felt as nervous as on the day of her first raid. All eyes were upon her.

Let me behave well, she thought. Let me act the part of a Crow chief.

A pipe was lit. She had never smoked, and she dreaded her turn. The pipe moved slowly from left to right around the circle of men. Nearer and nearer it came.

No word was spoken as the pipe was passed. Cheeks hollowed with long draws upon the stem. Solemn faces disappeared behind the puffs of smoke and reappeared shining with satisfaction.

I shall not cough, Lonesome Star vowed to herself. I shall not!

No one took more than three puffs, and the pipe moved closer with alarming speed. Suddenly she was holding it.

The advisors were watching. The warriors were watching. She knew her hand trembled. She was sure everyone saw the pipe shaking in her grasp.

She put the long, flat stem to her lips and drew. Her mouth filled with a hot, burning mixture of wild rose bark and tobacco. She clamped her teeth into the pipe stem.

Slowly she blew out smoke and passed the pipe. She had not coughed! A stirring, like a great sigh of relief, moved through the crowded lodge.

Lonesome Star sat in quiet triumph. There were speeches. Red Bull spoke of her courage and leadership. His words were repeated by other warriors who had served under her.

War Horse, who was leader of her military club, rose to his feet. He motioned Lonesome Star to do the same.

"From this day forward you shall sit among the chiefs in council," he said. "From this day forward you shall be called Woman Chief."

His voice was not loud. But it seemed to go all over the universe and fill it.

The men left the council lodge. Outside the women greeted them with the tremolo. A crier called everyone to Red Bull's lodge to eat wild-cherry pudding.

Woman Chief lifted her gaze to the skies. She remembered Sharp Knife's words of long ago.

Someday when you have performed great deeds, you shall have a new name, and it shall be honored among our people forever.

Around her she felt the mountains looking down, silently smiling on her.

9

Woman Chief was the only female ever to have a
regular place at council meetings.

Before long, her abilities thrust her even higher.
She rose to be third-ranking chief in her band of one
hundred sixty lodges.

The opportunity for leadership would have bypassed her had the Crows been a nation of farmers. But as they were a military people a good record in war ranked above all other virtues. Qualities such as intelligence and kindness, or the skills of storytelling and healing, were highly prized, but they lagged behind the highest merit, success as a warrior.

Woman Chief had achieved her ambitions. She had earned her honors and fame not by serving men, but by making room for herself at their side. But she never denied her womanhood—she glorified it, and an ever-present sign was her attire. Throughout her life she wore female garments only.

For a while she was content.

She still loved the hunt and the deadly sigh of the war lance. The hides she brought home she gave to Sharp Knife's family. The meat she cured and dried with the help of his children, who had been put in her charge.

But now she began to think more and more of possessions. Up to now whenever she had needed horses she had raided the enemy. She had kept only enough animals to use in trading for other necessities. Now she kept many for herself. They were the mark of wealth and power.

Since Sharp Knife's death she had ruled his lodge.

As a chief she wished for a lodge of her own. But no offer of marriage had been made by anyone.

"The young men admire you," Red Bull had once told her. "But they also fear you. They say you will be too difficult to manage as a wife."

During her younger days she had seldom thought about marriage. It was something that would happen in time. But many summers had gone by. Past thirty, she remained without a husband.

The horror of growing too old to hunt or raid haunted her. Would she finish her life in loneliness— a bent and stiff old woman good for nothing but to sleep by the tepee entrance and ward off dogs with a club?

The occasions to flirt were many, but Woman Chief would not play those games.

"I will not pretend to be shy," she told Little Feather. "I will be myself."

She would not fetch water, the lowliest of woman's work. So no youth waited in the bushes for her, ready to jump out and steal a hug.

She would not fell trees for tepee poles like other women. So no youth asked her to the mountains and trimmed her trees and dragged them home and touched her along the way.

She never went berry picking. Once, only once, had she been invited to gather wild rhubarb. Red Bull had taken her when they were both very young. He had apologized for fighting unfairly. That was all.

Red Bull had been married many summers, and one of his sons was nearly old enough to go on raids. Most of the playmates of her childhood had families. Even Little Dog, whom she had once thrown from his horse, had a big lodge filled with a wife and children though he had never taken a scalp.

In her own way Woman Chief now began to make her willingness known to suitors. When the camp moved, she rode apart.

The line of march was strung out for several miles. Daughters became separated from mothers, and the unwed braves seized the opportunity. They dressed in their finest clothes. In front of the girls they wanted they showed off their horsemanship and themselves.

Whenever traveling from campsite to campsite, Woman Chief played her lonely role. A brave could approach her. He could speak his heart without being overheard.

Through the spring and summer she hunted a husband. She persisted with the same iron will that had made her a better warrior than many men. Only now she was trying to be as good as a woman.

She would not act eager. She refused to lower herself to that. She simply let herself be counted among the unmarried women.

"Come, ride over," her tall figure said. "If you want me for your wife, woo me." No brave accepted the unspoken invitation.

The days grew colder. The band moved to the mountains to hunt. The leaves changed colors, crinkled, and fell.

"I shall try no more," she told Little Feather one day. "The men are afraid. They say I will bully my husband."

Little Feather was cutting forked sticks to make drying racks for meat. The hand holding the knife lowered.

"You can have your own lodge, and it need not be empty," she said in a small voice. "We are an understanding people."

If Little Feather's meaning was not stated outright, it was nonetheless clear. Woman Chief thought about it.

She remembered the moccasins Little Feather had made for her, and the elkskin dress she had trimmed with locks of hair. After all these years the beautiful maiden was unwed. How many handsome young men had she turned down because she loved a woman?

"I shall speak with your father," Woman Chief said at last. "My horses are many, and we shall hunt tomorrow. Where you slept, his lodge will be piled with hides."

Little Feather lifted her eyes and smiled. It was a smile that had been behind her lips many years, waiting.

"I shall make you a good wife," she said.

It was early winter, the time when the buffalo were sleek and fat and at their best. After obtaining the consent of Little Feather's father, the two women left the village together.

Woman Chief rode in front. Little Feather followed, leading a fast hunting horse. Early on the second day they came upon a herd of buffalo. The animals were feeding in scattered bunches.

Woman Chief rode onto a butte. She scanned the herd and singled out a group of about thirty.

Suddenly, beside her, Little Feather yelled, "*Yihoo!* Over there!"

Woman Chief looked where Little Feather pointed. She saw a huge buffalo. Its fur was a dirty cream color.

"A white buffalo!" cried Little Feather. "Do you see him?"

"Yes," replied Woman Chief, although she half doubted her own eyes. She immediately changed horses. "It is a good omen," she called, and rode like an arrow for the prize.

The white buffalo lifted his shaggy head and sniffed, his small weak eyes lost in the mop of hair. He seemed to sense death riding him down. He spun to flee.

The arrow struck him in the left shoulder. He lifted his front legs and gave a few startled jumps, but he did not go down.

You are a brave one, thought Woman Chief, riding so close to him that his blood flicked onto her thigh. She took a deep breath and released a second arrow. The white giant pitched forward headfirst. His body quivered. He snorted and kicked. After a moment he lay still.

Woman Chief dismounted. She stared at the great beast, marveling. There were many stories about sacred white buffalo. She had always thought them tales of long ago. Never before had she believed they were still true.

There was no time to allow herself more than a brief treat of staring and marveling. The herd showed signs of shifting. Already the buffalo nearest her were acting up. Their keen noses had smelled blood and the scent of the hunter. They trotted about, tails held high.

Woman Chief waited for the shifting to stop and the animals nearby to calm down. She did not want a stampede. Then she circled downwind.

Her expert eyes picked out cows rather than bulls. Cows' hides were easier to tan. They made better bed robes and tepee coverings. And it was hides she was hunting. Beautiful hides. Hides to give Little Feather's father.

She dodged among the buffalo tirelessly. A gun would have made it possible to kill from longer range. But she disliked guns. The thundering noises made a herd take flight.

Bow and arrow suited her. They were silent weapons, and no man handled them better. She cut down buffalo after buffalo without disturbing the rest of the herd.

When she had enough hides, she shouldered her bow. The afternoon was half gone. She rode to Little Feather and helped with the skinning. They worked together smoothly, rapidly.

Little Feather was an expert skinner. Her curved

knife slit and cut while the carcasses were still warm. Before the sun went down, they had removed almost all the hides.

"It has been a fine day," Little Feather said as darkness came on. She was butchering one of the buffalo for the evening meal.

"There is nothing left in the herd worth taking," replied Woman Chief with a hunter's pride.

"The skins are beautiful," agreed Little Feather. "Our people have learned well."

It was a remark typical of her. She was giving praise. Yet she was saying something more. What Little Feather was hinting at caught Woman Chief off guard, but she knew it was true. She had not hunted as an Indian. She had "learned well" the wants of the white men. The buffalo she had picked out to kill were mostly the white men's favorite colors—buckskin and beaver. Hides of these colors brought the best prices at the trading posts.

Woman Chief had not realized how much the white men had influenced her thinking. She felt a pang of shame. Her pleasure from the day's success was tarnished. She did not know how to reply to Little Feather. As a hunter and warrior, it was not in her nature to apologize or offer excuses. She fell back upon her role as provider. She gave Little Feather one of the hides. It was mouse-colored with a rich, bluish cast; not the white men's favorite color, but Little Feather's.

It was a gift of the heart, and it said, "Your head is wise. You will be good to have in my lodge."

Little Feather ran her hands over the fine, wavy fur and murmured her thanks. "I will tan it very soft," she said.

They camped another two days while Little Feather decorated the sacred white hide. When they departed, they left the hide on a hilltop as an offering to the sun.

The other hides Woman Chief took to the tepee where Little Feather lived. She also took seven war-horses.

Little Feather's father was well pleased. It was a handsome payment. In return, he let his daughter marry Woman Chief.

Several women made the couple a splendid tepee —so large it required twenty hides. When it was done, sagebrush and weeds were burned inside.

"This will keep out the rain," said one of the women, and she opened the smoke hole.

A dance was held within the new lodge. Afterward

the men sat around and puffed a pipe with Woman Chief.

"Be kind to her," said Little Feather's father, "and she will not run away."

10

The seasons changed. Time did not bring wrinkles to Woman Chief's face, but she felt the years deeply.

She had never been afraid or unkind. She still hunted with the skill of her youth. She was generous and saw that the old people and the needy had meat. She had taken three more wives over the years and thus added to her dignity as a chief; for after victories in war, wealth in women and horses marked a Crow warrior's standing in the band. She still led war parties.

Her way of life was fading, however.

Slowly but steadily the white men were breaking up the ancient Indian customs and habits. Though Woman Chief's face did not show the lines of age, her heart often pined for the old days, before the wagons and forts and riverboats. Somehow they were better.

But the threat of the white men to the Indians was still young. Although Woman Chief sensed the danger that the whites brought, she also felt they brought good. Their manufactured goods delighted her, and their admiration for her pleased her. Foreign visitors made a point of meeting her. She basked in their attention.

In 1851 Rudolph Kurz, a young Swiss artist, traveled west to paint Indians. He met the warrior-woman at Fort Union.

"She is modest in manner and good humored rather than quick to quarrel," he wrote in his diary.

The artist received a scalp she had taken in battle. Fascinated, he spent all his time interviewing her and never got around to painting her portrait. So, alas, the opportunity to record her likeness was lost.

Little Feather did not share Woman Chief's friendliness toward the white men.

"They are coming like the snow," she said. "They will bury us."

"You no longer have to twirl a fire drill," Woman Chief argued. "You have strike-alights. And is it not easier to cook in metal kettles than by dropping hot rocks into rawhide filled with water?"

"Yes," replied Little Feather. "And it is easier to embroider with colored glass beads than to get and dye porcupine quills."

"So be grateful to the whites," said Woman Chief.

"I would rather live as my grandmother lived," retorted Little Feather. "The white men will kill all the buffalo for the hides. They will destroy the forests and the grasslands. Hear me well. We will no longer be able to live by hunting. The Crows will become farmers or beggars."

"The buffalo will always cover the earth," said Woman Chief impatiently. "We need the white man. We are wealthier in horses than our enemies. But both the Blackfeet and the Sioux outnumber us three to one. We need the white man as our ally."

Nevertheless Woman Chief was bothered and upset by Little Feather's words. It was true that in increasing numbers the Crows were content to hang around the white men's forts. The old braves were becoming beggars, the old women thieves.

Woman Chief threw herself upon her bed of sleeping robes and stared moodily at a single star through the smoke hole. Little Feather came over and gently rubbed the soles of her feet with warm tallow.

"Perhaps you are right," said Woman Chief in a troubled whisper. "But what can be done?"

"The nations must join together," said Little Feather. "Together we can hold off the white men."

"Blackfoot and Sioux will never make peace with the Crow."

"Start with other nations," said Little Feather. "*Someone* must try to bring them together."

"And you wish that someone to be me?"

"Yes," said Little Feather. "There is nothing more within your power to gain among the Crows. You have standing, honor, and riches. Only two chiefs rank above you. You cannot hope to leap over them."

"I know," said Woman Chief. Little Feather had caused her to think once more about her two lifelong foes—her sex and her birth.

She had been born a girl and a Gros Ventre. Among the Crows she lacked family connections. To be head of the nation, or even of a band, a warrior needed the wide backing of many rich relatives.

How often she had reshaped the past in her thoughts! Had she not been captured, she might have been chief of a band of Gros Ventres. Perhaps chief of the whole nation, had she been born a boy!

To Little Feather she said, "My name is honored. My enemies fear me. I seek nothing higher."

"You must work to unite the nations," urged Little Feather. "You must *try!*"

Woman Chief closed her eyes. "I will think about it," she muttered.

But several moons passed, and she did nothing. Whenever Little Feather raised the subject, Woman Chief talked of other matters.

Then the camp received news. The white men wanted to meet with all the tribes of the upper Missouri River. Woman Chief went with six Crows to Fort Laramie. They signed a treaty.

Little Feather sneered at it.

"It is a white man's treaty," she scoffed. "Now they can build roads and soldier posts across our land. What has their paper given us?"

"The white men and the chiefs have made a lasting peace," Woman Chief said. "We will live together in friendship."

In the beginning it seemed she was right. The Blackfeet and a portion of the Gros Ventres of the Prairie even invited the Crows and the Assiniboins to visit them, sending friendly messages and talking of peace. The Crows were skeptical. After so many years of warfare could peace come so easily? But the Assiniboins accepted the Gros Ventres' invitation. They were entertained hospitably, and on leaving they were given horses as gifts.

The Gros Ventres and the Assiniboins continued to deal peacefully and profitably with one another for three years. But as yet the Crows had not gone to the camps of any of their former foes. Woman Chief began to think of opening the way.

"I was right about the treaty," she told Little Feather. "This is a lasting peace. It is wrong for the Crows not to participate in it. And we have need of horses, as well."

Woman Chief's own people were unwilling to encourage the undertaking. Several white traders attempted to talk her out of going. She was the wrong person, they said.

"Your feats against the Gros Ventres are too well known," one old fur trader warned. "The braves you killed are not easily forgotten."

Surprisingly even Little Feather voiced doubt about the wisdom of the trip. "I am afraid for you," she confessed. "A white man's treaty is only a piece of paper. It cannot erase the fact that you are an enemy of the Gros Ventres."

"I was born a Gros Ventre of the Prairie," Woman Chief reminded her. "They have been friendly to other old enemies. I can go among them without harm. And is it not as you wished?"

"My wish was that you start with friendlier nations," answered Little Feather.

In the fire in front of them a charred log broke and fell inward with a popping and snapping and a lovely shower of sparks.

"I have a dream that comes and goes," said Little Feather. "Always it is the same. If you go to that strange place, you will not come home to me ever again."

"I shall go," said Woman Chief. "Someone must learn the mood of the Gros Ventres and whether their hostility toward us has truly changed."

Little Feather trembled.

"I have thought long," Woman Chief said gently. "You were right. We cannot depend upon the whites. The line must be drawn between us and them or they will draw the line around us. If the nations stand together, we can renew everything as it was and make it better. Do not worry. I shall come back to you. It is just a dream."

Under a dark and gloomy sky Woman Chief began the dangerous journey. Four braves went with her. They were young, hanging between awkward boyhood and this chance for manly honors.

They had not traveled two days when a party of Gros Ventres crossed their path. The Gros Ventres were returning home from a trip to Fort Union and seemed friendly.

Woman Chief danced her horse across the open space between them. The Gros Ventres halted. A heavyset brave rode from the ragged column. "I am First Boy," he greeted her. "Welcome."

The other Crows rode up. First Boy motioned his people to relax. He scanned the surrounding countryside before deciding upon a place to talk.

The spot he selected, a crooked shoulder of rock enclosing a space big enough for ten or twelve people, was on the way to the Gros Ventres' camp. Woman Chief did not like it. But she put aside her misgivings rather than offend First Boy by objecting.

A fire was lit. The five Crows sat down in a circle with seven Gros Ventres. Soon they were smoking and talking.

Woman Chief explained the reason for her journey.

"Before the treaty at Fort Laramie, scarcely six sunsets passed without large numbers of horses being swept off by war parties. Men were killed, and their deaths cried for revenge," she said. "Now we have peace. But it is a peace that profits the white man more than it profits us. The buffalo become fewer each day. Let us make a lasting peace without the white men. A peace among brothers."

First Boy took a thoughtful drag on the pipe.

"It is strange," he said, "that a woman is sent on so important a mission."

"I am a chief of the Crows," Woman Chief replied.

"Woman Chief?" he said. "You are she?"

His tone was even, but his eyes were suddenly busy among the Crows.

"Many of our proudest warriors have fallen by your hand," he said. "It is good that we sit together and talk of peace."

Woman Chief knew she must leave quickly. First Boy had risen. He was whispering to one of his braves. The man ran off.

"Do not be uneasy," said First Boy. "I sent him after the horses. Your words are good. I shall carry them to my people."

The Crows' horses were led forth, along with twelve others.

"Strong, fast horses," said First Boy. "Take them. Tell all the Crows that we wish peace also."

Each Crow brave was given his own horse and two as gifts. Woman Chief received four.

They are facing the wrong way . . .

The thought darted across Woman Chief's mind as, mounting, she had to turn her back on the Gros Ventres.

She had a fleeting glimpse of her four Crows. Their faces were fixed with dread.

All motion seemed to freeze with their expressions. The world stopped as it had stopped long ago. In a flash of recall, she was a little girl carrying a dead bird to Grandfather's lodge, moments before her village was destroyed.

The war whoops of her memory mingled with those in her ears. The air hissed with arrows.

Suddenly the Crow braves were lying on the ground. Woman Chief was bleeding and could not breathe.

More arrows struck her.

She drew her knife as she sank. She tried to twist and face the treachery, but could not. The knife slipped from her fingers. She fell forward, her cheek rubbing along the belly of her horse.

She lay on the ground and stared at the sun. Then her eyes closed, and she knew no more forever.

Epilogue

The murder of Woman Chief inflamed the Crow nation and cries for vengeance shattered any chance for peace.

Search parties were sent to recover her body. It was never found.

Little Feather watched the last searchers returning.

A heavy rain was falling. The braves sat on their horses wet and miserable, huddled together under their robes.

It does not matter where her body rests, thought Little Feather. It is but dust.

She lifted her head and bared her face to the rain. In a while the sky would clear, the storm would pass.

She is the light that burns in every woman, thought Little Feather. She is the pride and the glory we hope for. She has not died.

Rose Sobol was born in The Bronx, New York, and received her B.A. from Brandeis University. She has worked as an engineer and computer programmer and is currently a part-time librarian in Miami, Florida. She coauthored *Stocks and Bonds* with her husband, Donald J. Sobol, who is the author of many books for young people.

Mrs. Sobol is currently involved in writing a humorous biography and studying ceramics.

F   **Sobol, Rose**
SOB
       Woman Chief

DATE			
	4-5		
1-3	Julle	S.	6-m
1-17	renew		6-m
1-31	renew	CS.	6-m
6-4	Brandy T		6-m